Marston & Me

Thomas Burtis

Pharos Books

ISBN: 978-93-67008-82-9
eISBN: 978-93-59837-06-2

©Publishers

Publisher: **Pharos Books (P) Ltd.**
Plot No.-63, First Floor, Main Mother Dairy Road
Pandav Nagar, East Delhi-110092
Phone: +14049995474, 011-40395855
WhatsApp: +91 9319228272
E-mail: sales@pharosbooks.in
Website: www.pharosbooks.in
Edition: 2024

Printed By: Sushma Book Binding House, Okhla
Industrial Area, Phase II, New Delhi-110020

Marston and Me
By : Thomas Burtis

I

Author of "Groody Among the Gushers," "The Lone Raider," etc.

Life on the border had hit a dry spell for some unknown reason. Not a —— thing had happened, was happening or seemed about to happen. For approximately four months the border patrolmen, of which, at times, I had the honor to be one, were slowly dying of dry-rot. We galloped up and down the frisky Rio Grande from Brownsville to San Diego, including waystations, with our customary eagerness to spot something of interest in connection with smuggling, rustling and other diversions of the Spigs and American renegades, but we were like a bunch of mosquitoes sucking on a piece of marble.

The McMullen flight, which I decorated with my lanky presence, was composed of youths like "Sleepy" Spears, "Tex" MacDowell and other flyers whose ideas of life do not include monotony as an ingredient of Paradise, and we were beginning to discuss the fact that the border was becoming really disgustingly effete. As Sleepy Spears put it in his slow drawl:

"The —— of it is that there's getting to be so —— much law down here they'll be sending delegations from Connecticut, Michigan and the Oneida Community to study Sheriff Bill Trowbridge's methods, and we might lose our jobs!"

All of which just goes to show that it is darkest just before you switch on the electric lights, and that it's a long worm which has no turning.

When the big news struck us we needed it, and I needed it most of all. It was the day after St. Patrick's day, and when I awakened to greet the morning after in Laredo I was sleeping in an alley, and alongside me was Lieutenant George Groody, at that time one of the leading lights of the American Air Service.

Groody had invited me, two days before, to participate in his annual celebration of St. Patrick's birthday.

"As an enemy of snakes," stated Groody, "Old Pat deserves the consideration of every true Irishman."

After the day was done I agreed, because I was on the verge of seeing a private collection of nice pink and blue ones myself. How was I to know that Groody invariably started St. Patrick's day in Mexico by ordering six gin fizzes set up in a row, and, starting with this little eye-opener, proceeding on to drinks adjacent? At midnight of the holiday we were drinking to Clemenceau, Lafayette and Garibaldi, having long before run out of dead flyers, movie stars and famous Irishmen.

Anyway, as I sent my De Haviland staggering on its way back to McMullen I was, temporarily, a prohibitionist, with particular reference to *tequila* and *mescal* and *aguadiente*, which are Mexican beverages guaranteed to grow hair on the top of Mt. Everest. Any one of the three will make a rabbit spit in a bulldog's face.

The airdome at McMullen is small, flat and hard to land on without over-running. I made it by a miracle, and as I stalked into headquarters I was greeted by a very perspicacious and inquiring look from the good eye of Cap Kennard, our genial flight commander.

"And did you enjoy yourself, 'Slim'?" he inquired, while "Pop" Cravath, our superannuated adjutant, laughed raucously.

"Temporarily," I admitted.

"Think you're going to bed now, put icebags on your head and tomatoes in your stomach, and convalesce?" pursued Kennard, his scarred face holding a peculiar expression.

He's been in twenty-three airplane wrecks, and what he did to the ships was as nothing to what he had done to his face.

Judging from photos of our stocky, chipper little C. O., he had joined the Air Service as a handsome young man with a face which could pass in a crowd on a dark night without sending any damsel into hysterics. After a couple of years in France and more time on the border, however, he looked as if he were breaking in a new pan for somebody else.

"What's up, Cap?" I demanded, being able to see through a ladder if some one lends me his glasses.

"The chief's got his bill through Congress, the bombing tests on those German battleships are going to take place this summer, and you, Slim, are ordered immediately to Langham Field, Virginia. You're going in advance of the picked flyers who'll drop the said bombs upon the bodies and persons of the Ostfriesland and other boats, and you've got to be out of here on the four o'clock train to San Antonio. Get under a cold shower, take some salts, drink a lot of icewater, pack the extra sock of yours, and may —— have mercy on your soul!"

II

All of which more or less accounts for the fact that I, Slim Evans in person, was ensconced on the edge of Chesapeake Bay three days later. Langham Field is in the commonwealth of Virginia with the bay bounding one edge of it. All around it on the other sides there are marshes and estuaries and swamps and puddles and so forth.

The mosquitoes have a formal review each night, and march and countermarch up and down any face within reach. Every once in a while there comes an order for them to take careful aim and fire. The first night I spent in the officers' barracks I had no screens on my windows, and the mosquitoes were so thick that when I started to throw my shirt in a corner it just hung right in the air.

Seriously speaking, I was in a very pleasant frame of mind at that, and I wouldn't be far wrong if I said that just about every other flyer in the service was in a similar mental condition. Granting, of course, that any man who flies for a living has any mind at all to be in any condition whatever.

The facts were that for weary months General Mallory, the chief, had been lifting his melodious voice to high heaven, Congress and the world at large, insisting that a bunch of airplanes flying out to sea with bombs aboard could considerably embarrass any navy approaching our shores. The fact that I was at Langham Field was simply due to the fact that Congress had finally taken a few dollars out of the appropriation for a new post office with a solid gold cupola for the town of Four Forks, Arkansas, and added it to the money which had been set aside to dredge the Yahee River in Mississippi and turned it over to the Air Service. The latter money was made available when the Yahee turned out to be a brook which had temporarily dried up.

The Air Service, I already knew, had developed a four thousand pound bomb, but the dope was that for the tests mere peas, as it were, weighing only two thousand pounds, would be used. It was the general's contention, which seemed to the naked eye to be well-founded, that a few of these eggs, each with a yolk consisting of a thousand pounds of T. N. T., when laid alongside a battleship might embarrass it a trifle.

In fact, he had an idea that said monarch of the seas might become extinct almost immediately. It meant plenty for the Air Service if they could prove that they could fly a hundred miles or so out to sea and bother a navy. And when one gets down to hardpan, every flyer I ever knew has a certain pride in his corps which is seldom equaled and never surpassed in any organization I know, from the Independent Order of Odd Fellows to the Queen's Own Royal Mounted Sussex Fusileers, which organization acts as bodyguard to the Prince of Wales, I understand, and have heavy casulaties daily as men die of heart failure, trying to follow him around.

I had but vague ideas of just what the plans were, and least of all as to why I had been ordered on ahead, until I reported to Major Lamb Johnson next morning. Major Lamb Johnson is a fox-faced little fellow with a spike mustache consisting of five hairs on one side and four on the other. He has a habit of blowing frequently with a loud report, and when he comes down to earth again the second lieutenants can be found fainting on the ground all around him.

He was striding up and down his office when I entered. From the windows of it I could see the long line of huge, corrugated iron hangars which bounded the southern edge of the field, and the one huge dirigible hangar on the northern side. Eastward was Chesapeake Bay, and on the western boundary were a few more hangars and some frame administration buildings.

"Come in, Evans," stated the Major. "You are here a month and a half before the hundred-odd picked veterans of the service arrive to commence practising for the bombing tests. The reason for your orders is that we want you as a ferry pilot. Your job will be to commute between here and Cleveland, Ohio, where the Martin factory is located, flying a new twin-motored Martin bomber to Langham each trip. Have you ever flown one?"

I shook my head.

"We have two on the field now, and Captain Lawton will teach you. You had a lot of big ship experience in France, I believe, and you also were officer-in-charge of ferrying three tankwings from Long Island to Texas a year or so ago, were you not?"

I agreed to this without reservation.

"The big ship squadron will be the 114th to which you'll be assigned immediately. Captain Lawton in command. It's just a skeleton squadron until the other flyers arrive, of course. Report to him immediately. Just one thing more, Evans."

I knew something was coming. Major Lamb was always full of good advice and uplifting thoughts.

"I have never served in the same outfit with you. However, your reputation is that of a flyer who gets where he's going by hook or crook, but that as an officer you are somewhat lax and careless. We are face to face with the biggest opportunity the service has ever had. Every man must put his shoulder to the wheel and live, think and breathe nothing but these tests, working twenty-four hours a day if necessary and——"

He went on with his discourse for some five minutes for the good of my soul and the glory of ——. At the end I expected that he'd lead in prayer for my unregenerate soul or something. Finally I got out after agreeing piously with everything he'd said and resolving to lead a better life.

Then I hied me up to the ten big hangars which were to house the 114th, and found old Cap Lawton, who's three inches over six feet and hence only a couple of inches shorter than I. In lankiness we are about alike, but whereas his feet are bigger than mine, my nose makes his seem like merely a microscopic growth in the middle of his thin face.

I knew him well, and he greeted me with a broad smile as he shook hands. After fanning a while I found out that my teammate in trips from Cleveland to Langham would be Les Fernald. We'd ferry two ships at a time.

"You'll be in command of Flight Three of the squadron, Slim, after the ships get here and the boys come in. At present that flight's got one sergeant first class in charge, and two mechanics. Later it'll have four sergeants, meaning one crew chief apiece for the ships, and eight mechanics. Your flight sergeant is Marston, a good man, although peculiar. Better stroll down and get acquainted with him, eh? You'll probably use him as mechanic on these trips of yours."

I strolled down to hangar fourteen which, it seemed, was to house the ships of Flight Three for the summer, and heard voices from the little tool room partitioned off in one corner of said iron structure. There wasn't a ship in the flight, of course, so the mechanics were about as busy as so many Congressmen.

As I approached the door there cut through the murmur of talk a loud, vulgar voice, heavy as lead, deep as the guile of the heathen Chinee and rough as a Texas boulevard. Unless I was badly mistaken, those vocal cords belonged to nobody but Major

George William Marston, and Georgy stood about as high in my estimation as a rattlesnake, and that's right on the ground.

I wondered what in —— he was doing at Langham Field. I hadn't heard his name mentioned. It made the summer prospect look very dark, not to say drear. Add George William to a field which Lamb Johnson was already cluttering up with his presence, and you've got a madhouse made to order for any godly young flyer.

George William had been only a first lieutenant when I was one of the scared, diffident young cadets whose lives were made miserable because they stood in constant threat of discharge, and discharge meant that the dream of a lifetime, to fly, was shattered as completely as a glass dropped off the top floor of the Woolworth building.

George William had been in charge of the cross-country stage, and he did his —— to get me kicked out because I was an hour late on making Seguin, the town I was bound for on my first cross-country trip. I got lost—sure. But I found my course again and I got there.

He disliked me primarily because I am physically, mentally and spiritually unable to feel as if any man who ranks me is automatically first assistant to ——, and one day when he called me a fighting name I took the opportunity to interview him alone and notify him sincerely that the next time he got personal with me I'd endeavor earnestly to hang his nose approximately under his left ear and do a quick job of rough and ready plastic surgery on his entire face.

He had been an old army sergeant, and he was a twenty-minute egg with a yolk made of gall and wormwood and an idea that saluting and saying "sir" were the ends and objects of a cadet's existence.

In a group of kiwis—the kiwi is a mythical Australian bird which has wings but can't fly—who were jealous of flyers and made their lives miserable, he was the *non plus ultra*, the *sine qua non* and likewise anything else which you can think of abutting closely on a total loss.

Well, I had become a full-fledged officer since then, so I ambled in that little tool room. There were two privates sitting there, and a sergeant. And the sarge was none other than my old friend, George William Marston!

I shouldn't be surprized if I swayed lightly on my feet—a mere suggestion of being knocked slightly off my pins. There he was, same as before—fleshy, dark face, pop eyes of light blue, three creases between his brows and deep-cut lines through the fat around his mouth. He looked more sullen than ever, and his black hair was much thinner.

If I was knocked for a row of Abyssinian applejack barrels, he was at least three laps ahead of me. Just as an ungodly feeling of joy and well-being went frolicking through my hardening arteries, his mouth was working spasmodically in an endeavor to say something. He had leaped to his feet like a shot, the other two being a split-second behind him, and he stood there as stiff as I was at my first Fireman's Grand Supper Entertainment and Ball back in Utah, where I originated.

"Rest!" I grinned, as the two soldiers relaxed.

But not Marston. He was unable to do anything momentarily.

In a flash I grasped the explanation. Marston had been made an officer from a sergeant during the war, and undoubtedly, when the regular army was formed from the temporary troops, he had been unable to pass the exams on such military matters as Latin, English literature and the biennial theorem. Consequently he, like many others, went back to his former grade.

"So you're a sergeant now, and you're to be my flight sergeant all summer!" I observed pleasantly.

How I was going to pay him back for days of mental agony was making a new man of me as I stood and looked at him. You may, brethren, give vent to several loud, uncultivated snorts at the idea of me being in mental agony about anything. To tell the truth,

I figured when I was a cadet that the country might struggle along without me in the flying corps, and I didn't give three whoops in hallelujah whether or not I was an officer.

But I did want to fly, and I wanted to get to France, and I didn't care whether or not I was carrying gold bars on my shoulders or a corporal's stripes on my sleeve. Any man who wanted to be an officer could go to a training camp and get the commission in three months. It took a lucky flyer six months and a few broken bones to get his.

Any man who became a flying cadet had his mind set on flying, and George William Marston was the nastiest, meanest obstacle in the way I had ever come across. He gave an order in a way that made it sound like an insult. And he seemed to take delight in rubbing our noses, particularly mine, in the dirt and then trying to discharge us if we objected to the smell. Of course, my nose was unduly prominent. Gents, he sure rode me into the ground.

"I'll be your flight commander all summer," I told the congregation. "You can go now—you two. I want to converse in private with Sergeant Marston."

The two privates filed out silently. Marston was still standing as if concrete had set in his backbone.

"Sit down, Major," I told him, and I'll swear the "Major" just slipped out naturally.

He relaxed, but did not subside on the tool chest next to him. His eyes, which popped out so far they could have been knocked off with a stick, met mine steadily. We had instinctively hated each other, I think, from the first time we met.

"Well, this is a rather peculiar situation, Marston," I told him as I ignited a cheroot. "The man that tried to break me is now under me."

"And about to be broken himself," Marston interrupted me.

His face seemed to me to have changed since the time I had seen him before. He looked as if he'd gone through —— and had become a sullen enemy of life in general. His light blue eyes, staring into mine, were glowing dully. He seemed to be daring me to do my worst as he looked at me.

And all of a sudden I hated myself because I had even considered using my strategic position to get back at him for what he had done to me.

"No, you're not going to be broken, Marston," I told him as he stood there like a lion at bay.

He simply looked at me, without saying a word. My particular and peculiar type of beauty did not appeal to him at all, and as for him, I didn't like anything about him and never had. In a personal sense, I mean.

"You can make my life a —— on earth, of course," he said after a lengthy silence. His voice had a deep husk in it.

"Sure," I agreed. "Listen, Marston. You always were a good soldier, as far as I know; leaned over backward to live up to regulations, and a hound on discipline. But you were without exception the rottenest officer I ever saw, and the nastiest and most unfair man a poor cadet ever had over him. You were enough all by yourself to ruin the morale of every cadet at Donovan Field. You'll make a —— sight better sergeant than you did an officer."

"And you were about the funniest sample of a soldier that any army, including the Mexican, ever had," he told me doggedly, and in his brooding light eyes that glow burned brighter. "You came lounging in as though you didn't give a —— for any orders or discipline whatever, and tried to do just what you —— pleased. And you're no more an army man right now than you were before.

"Oh, I've heard plenty about you. You've pulled off a few good flying stunts, but you're not a soldier and never will be. And by —— if you think I'm going to lick your boots because you, a young squirt who never had any responsibility about him, is an officer and I'm only a sergeant——"

"Pull in your neck, Marston; you're stretching it," I advised him. "You'd better thank your lucky stars that I'm not going to try to get even with you for what you put me through. I'm a flyer now, but I can still look back at the months when I was bound up in the effort to get to be a flyer, and the stuff you put me through.

"But Marston, I'm going to relieve the spleen that's gathered in my system. As long as you're under me you soldier as you never did before. I'll show you no favors, but I'll not pick on you until you slip. Then you're going to get it right in the neck. Meanwhile, Marston, do you remember the day just before inspection when you dressed me down in front of the troops, and called me a nice, pretty name which cast certain aspersions on my ancestry?"

He stood there and said nothing, but the ferocious gleam in his eyes said plenty. No doubt he had brooded for years after slipping back from the grade of major to that of sergeant. Some drop, I'll say.

"We're quiet and alone, Marston. Temporarily I'm taking off these pretty little collar ornaments, and forgetting that I'm a looey in this man's army. And I'm going to beat you half to death, —— willing, as between man and man. And whoever wins, we'll walk out of here and the past'll be forgotten as long as you're a soldier."

He hesitated briefly.

"If I beat you up, Evans, I'll pay through the nose for it. You've got all summer to pay me up for a fight, and you'll do it. I can't win."

"You button up your mouth, Marston," I told him grimly. "Don't judge me or any other man by your own standards. I don't even want to kid myself by pretending that I could ride you all summer for personal reasons and then excuse myself by saying that you need discipline. I wouldn't be that low, but that's what you did. Get that shirt off, if you want to, and put up your hands. The personal representative of several thousand cadets whose lives you made miserable, including several dozen that you got kicked out entirely, is standing right in front of you."

"And is going to get the beating of his life!" bellowed Marston suddenly.

He tore off his O. D. shirt as if possessed. All the accumulated bitterness of the last couple of years, I imagine, added to the natural meanness in him, broke through the dam and turned him into a fighting fool.

He weighed as much as I did, but I was a foot taller and my reach was many inches greater than his. As he came toward me joyfully he sent his powerful, stocky body at me like a cannon ball. I sidestepped, and got in a peach right to the button.

It is not my intention to give a round-by-round story of the battle. I couldn't. It was too fast and much too furious. We were fighting, remember, in a little tool-room, impeded by toolchests, and with rows of shelves around the walls filled with wrenches, cotter pins and all sorts of spare parts. I didn't have room enough to dance around and keep him out of reach, and he took blow after blow in order to get into very close quarters.

I floored him in the first ten seconds, but he was back on his feet as if he'd bounced off the floor. Once again he came hurtling in, and again I dropped him. His nose was bleeding profusely, not to say fluently by that time, but he was strong as a bull. The next time in he ducked a hurried right swing which I started from the floor, and the next instant we went crashing against the shelves. With a powerful heave he threw me to the floor, and for about a half minute we fought like wildcats all over the place. He used his feet, too, but luckily I got out of his gorilla-like grip in time and up to my feet.

The next minute or so is just a crimson-tinted haze as far as I'm concerned. We stood toe to toe and swapped blows. Twice he got me to the floor again, and in a brief interval when I kept him away from me, I floored him once more.

He came up more slowly, and I leaped in with a one-two punch that I traded for a trip-hammer swing that caught me just under the ear. I went spinning against a tool chest, and fell over it with a crash just as he dropped himself. I was dazed, dizzy, and somewhat, if not entirely, *non compos mentis* for a moment.

As I tried to clear my head and get to my feet I saw him getting up groggily. Before I could get further than my knees he hurled himself across that tool chest and on top of me, his huge fingers clutching blindly for my throat.

I felt as if I were fighting in a dream, and for my life or something. What brought me to, paradoxically enough, was a glancing blow from a light wrench. In a second my mind snapped to attention, and for a moment I was a strong man as I saw myself knocked out with a piece of iron. He had evidently grabbed the wrench from one of the shelves as I fell over the chest.

With feet and fists flying so fast they must have looked like a spinning pinwheel, I threw him off, and staggered to my feet. I gave him no quarter. He had trouble getting up for a minute. I had one of his eyes closed and his head was none too clear. He hadn't got across the tool chest before I socked him a beauty, and he went crashing against the shelves.

Staggering and dizzy as I was, I had enough left. His hands dropped helplessly, and I lifted him about two inches off the floor and deposited him four feet away and flat on his back with a roundhouse swing. Between measuring, getting my arm back and smacking him he had time enough to light a cigaret and smoke it, but he was too weak and blind and dazed and whatever else a man is when he's out on his feet, even to block it. Maybe he didn't see it. Anyway, he saw stars a minute later.

He lay on the floor, unable to move but not mentally out. I parked myself on a tool chest, and devoted my exclusive attention to inhaling large gobs of air into my laboring lungs. No use of talking, I was getting soft at that period. A little scrap got me gasping like Paul Revere's horse.

Finally I was able to light a cigaret, and as its soothing flavor was beginning to permeate the stuffy air of the tool room my dear friend Marston rose on his hind legs and peered at me through one good eye which, it appeared to me, needed the ministrations of some good raw steak to save him from becoming temporarily blind.

"Now that I've relieved myself, I feel better," I informed him.

"Didn't think you had it in you," he barked, his ordinarily husky voice deeper than usual. "I thought you lacked a punch—in anything."

"Your opinion of me was low in all particulars," I grinned. "As for me, I thought that when your bars were gone you had nothing left."

"Well, you licked me," he stated, hate peering forth from the one slit in his face which remained of two eyes. "And I s'pose this is just the start of what I'll go through. You——"

"Shut up,——you!" I snapped. "That's about the last time you'll insinuate that I'm as low as you were when you had a commission, or I'll put you out of your misery *pronto* and all you'll have to worry about is whether you fry in —— or merely stew."

He said nothing, but applied a dirty handkerchief tenderly to his nose. The wrinkles between his black, bushy brows were deeper than ever, and his face was so sullen it was black.

"One thing more I desire to converse with you about, Marston," I went on after my temper was in control. "Captain Lawton implied to me that you were a good mechanic."

"You're —— right, I'm a good mechanic."

"My job is to ferry Martin Bombers from Cleveland to Langham for the next month. Want to be my mechanic? I'm not asking you for the pleasure of your company, you may be sure, but you're supposed to be the best motor man in the squadron."

"And being under you or with you isn't no pleasant prospect for me," he told me, stubborn and unafraid. "But I go where I'm ordered."

"You'll make some extra dough out of your travel allowance, you may enjoy the trip, and there are about two hundred mechanics on the field would give their shirts to go," I told him. "Likewise, I hate to take you worse than poison. But you're the best man, and you can just paste it in your hat that you're having the first illustration of the fact that you'll get a square deal around here when I say that you'll be ordered to go along."

He grunted, squinting up at me balefully.

"Another thing, Marston," I told him as I got up to go. "We've laid aside rank and that stuff for a while. But remember, now that our personal affairs are adjusted, that I'm wearing a commission and you're a sergeant. Say 'sir' to me, Marston, and don't ever presume to forget that you're a soldier and I'm an officer."

He laughed—a raucous series of cachinnations which had often impinged against my eardrums unpleasantly.

"You talkin' to me about bein' a soldier. Very well, sir!"

"Our travel orders should be out in a day or two. Be ready."

"Yes, sir."

"Go over to the hospital, get those shiners fixed up, report back and we'll go over the tools and other junk of the flight."

"Yes, sir."

And that was that. I told Lawton I'd take Marston for mechanic, and next day travel orders for Lieutenants Evans and Fernald, and Sergeants Marston and Bailey arrived in our respective boxes. The evening of the second day following Fernald and I met our non-coms at the Martin factory in Cleveland for a look-see at the ships.

III

You've probably heard heard of Les Fernald. He was on the round-the-world flight. He was a powerful, well-built chap of medium height with a pair of steady eyes, a nice smile, and the ability to fly a big ship about as well as it is given to man or beast to do anything. He'd had a lot of experience on Martins, whereas I only had a test flight with Lawton before I left. But I'd had some Caproni flying over in dear old France on some of my days away from Paris, and I'd lumbered through the ozone between Long Island and Texas with a three-motored Tankwing under me.

Out at the factory late that afternoon the two mechanics and ourselves inspected the ships, and then Fernald and I flew them on a test flight. They ticked away like clocks, and were perfectly rigged. I took Marston along on the flight, and he nodded his satisfaction to me at the same time that his rainbow-hued eyes glowed his dislike into my own.

We landed again on the private flying field of the factory and announced that we'd leave early next morning. So saying, we hied ourselves down to a hostelry while the mechanics got the ships gassed, oiled and ready to ramble. They were to be stabled for the night in a canvas hangar at the edge of the factory flying field.

At our early breakfast next morning a headline caught my eye, and as a result a scalding gulp of coffee went down the wrong tunnel. The java ended up in my right lung, I think, and I coughed enough to make the citizens of Cleveland think the lake breeze had become very strong all of a sudden.

"Listen, Les," I said at length, wiping the tears from my eyes. "'HANGAR ON MARTIN FLYING FIELD BURNED. Two Martin Bombers, VALUED AT $100,000, COMPLETELY DESTROYED.'"

If you told Les Fernald that the continent of Europe had sunk into the sea, and that North America was expected to follow it into the briny deep, he'd probably say:

"Well, let's improve the time we've got left and see a good show, or have a drink or something."

So the rise I got out of him was:

"Read on, Slim. You interest me."

The story, peeled down to the core, was simply that the two ships we were to fly to Langham that day had been burned up, that no one could figure how the fire had started, and that the entire factory had been in great danger of ignition, so to speak. Only herculean efforts had saved it. Three fires, at different points, had been discovered before they got burning merrily enough to be out of control.

We cantered out to the factory without delay, and found a very mystified bunch of men, from the G. M. down. The only possible explanation they had for it was that a group of ten workmen had been fired a few weeks after the discovery that they were grafting, and that possibly they had started the conflagration to get revenge. We wired Washington, and were ordered to stay in Cleveland a few days until the next two Martins were ready. The factory schedule on the army contract was four ships a week.

Marston poked around in his sullen, scowling way, and when I ran across him out at the excited factory I inquired casually:

"Did you happen to see the fire? We were in bed early and never knew it until this morning."

"No, sir. I was in bed before midnight."

Which proved to be an unadulterated lie. Fifteen minutes later I overheard Bailey—this was out at the factory—say to Marston—

"Well, did you tear the town loose last night?"

"Nah—nothing doing," rasped Marston in return.

There was nothing for us to do at the factory—they were all running around ragged out there anyway—so as we left it I herded Bailey to one side. Marston had left by himself, but I wanted the conversation to be private.

"Marston living with you?" I asked him.

"Yes, sir," said the slim young Bailey.

"He was out late last night, was he?"

"Yes, sir. About three A. M."

"I see. Just wanted to know. Come in drunk?"

Bailey was troubled. He didn't want to tell tales, I could see. So I went on:

"Don't be scared to tell me. I just don't want Marston to be in bad shape for the trip."

"He wasn't, sir. He'd been drinking, but he wasn't drunk."

"Thanks. That's all."

I wondered why George William had lied about being in bed early. It was a senseless thing to do. Not that I connected him with the fire at all, of course. But I was just curious. He went around with a chip balanced precariously on his shoulder all the time, that was sure, and seemed to crave no company of any kind whatever. The only reason he lived with Bailey at all, I presume, was to save money.

It worried me a little, taking it by and large. Finally, as we reached our palatial suite of two rooms and connecting bath in the most ornate hostelry in Cleveland, I put it up to Fernald. He knew the history of Marston and me.

"Why do you suppose he lied?" I asked him.

"Probably thought it was none of your business where he was last night," Fernald grinned.

"In which assumption," I admitted, "he would be entirely correct. But, the question once asked, there was no reason———"

"Except that he is as fond of you as a bull is of a red kimono," Les reminded me. "Well, let's step out and see the town."

IV

During the ensuing three days we saw plenty of it, and finally went through the procedure of inspecting and testing two more Martins. By this time the Martin factory was under heavy guard. The Martins being vitally important—in fact, indispensable—for the conduct of the bombing tests, the company was under a heavy forfeit clause in the contract for twenty thereof, and the mere idea that there was dirty work at the cross-roads struck them with panic.

Detectives were rounding up the discharged and discredited employees little by little and each by each. So far no confession had been third-degreed out of the men. The first lot all had alibis.

Believe me, though, we inspected the ships from stem to stern and from rudder to nose again the next morning before we started on our way. Our route lay over the flat Ohio fields, almost due south to McCook Field at Dayton. There we gassed up, and set sail eastward to Boundville, which is a West Virginia village right on the bank of the Ohio River in that little sliver of West Virginia which hides coyly between Ohio and Pennsylvania. At Boundville the government maintains a little way-station on the Washington-Dayton airway. It's just a field with a few spare parts and some gas and oil available.

It was a nice trip.

In case you don't know a Martin, let me elucidate a bit for thee. The ship weighs four tons, and has about seventy feet of wingspread. On each wing, just far enough from the cockpit to allow the propellers to whirl without hitting anything, a Liberty motor is set in a maze of huge, trunklike struts which hold it up and in and down; in fact, keep it safely anchored.

The pilot's cockpit, with two seats side by side in it, is set a bit forward of the wings, about on a line with the two propellers in front of the motors. Ahead of the pilot's cockpit, in the very nose of the ship, is an observer's cockpit, equipped with bomb-sights, glass in the flooring to look down through, bomb releases, and about a thousand other things with technical names as long as your arm, or even as long as mine, which is considerably lengthy.

Directly in back of the pilot's cockpit, in the fore part of the huge fuselage, is the hollow bomb compartment, with bomb racks which can carry two tons of bombs, ranging from a swarm of little twenty-five pounders up through three hundreds, six hundreds, two one-thousand pounders or one two-thousand baby.

In back of this compartment, about half way to the tail surfaces, there is a cockpit for the mechanic or radio operator. The tail surfaces consist of elevators, vertical fin and stabilizer, each very large, but otherwise the same as in any ship, and it has two big rudders, both worked by the same rudder bar.

Les and I, like fleas on elephants' backs, set our course from Dayton to a bit south of the airline to make sure. When we sighted the wide, sluggish-looking Ohio we simply flew up the stream until the field at Boundville came in sight.

It's somewhat of a trick to land a Martin, because you've got two motors to handle, the ship is so heavy that it settles rapidly, and the pilot's cockpit is about ten feet above the ground. That makes leveling off a foot above the ground a bit difficult, at first. I made it the first try by bull luck in that small field, and Les did it with nonchalant ease, of course.

Marston had been riding alongside me the whole trip looking straight ahead and not vouchsafing me so much as a look, either dirty or otherwise. He and I exchanged as few words as the law allowed. The cars from town commenced to arrive immediately, of course, to look over the huge ships which were so awe-inspiring compared to the De Havilands the townspeople were accustomed to. There was one lonesome soldier in charge of the gas and oil.

We were to spend the night there, there being no wild rush. We taxied the ships up to the line in front of the gas shack, turned them around, and climbed out after running out the motors.

"Both of you stay here until the ships are gassed and oiled, and until dark, when the people quit coming," I told them. "This trip you, Marston, will spend the night out here on guard, and next trip Bailey can take it. That suit you, Les?"

"Sure," returned that young gentlemen. "At that, Bailey, 'd advise you to stay out here rather than in the one hotel down there. It's name ought to be the 'Bedbug's Roost,' and it has the first collection of bowls and pitchers and other sanitary brica-brac I've seen since the hogs ate my brother."

Bailey, one of the clean-looking, bright youngsters who came into the army during the war and stayed, grinned and allowed that he'd try it. Les and I accepted a ride into town with our baggage after I'd made arrangements with the soldier on duty to supply Marston with blankets. George William set to work bleakly, not uttering so much as a word. He would be out there all alone, because the field guard's duty did not include night work.

We saw a wild western movie called "Temptations of the Flesh," fought off curious questioners the whole length of the one street, and retired early because there was nothing else to do. It was the sort of a town I'd like to come to after a month of ribaldry, to settle down for a week or two and do nothing but drink Pluto and watch the sun go down.

Our start was planned for seven o'clock, and we were out there right on time. We wanted to cross the towering Cumberlands of West Virginia early, before it got hot and the cañons and rivers and woods and rocks made the air too bumpy.

Early as we were, however, a parade of cars followed us out. The residents of Boundville considered eleven A. M. the middle of the night, and four was the fashionable breakfast hour. As our Ford bumped into the field, leading a miscellaneous collection of vehicles, I spotted Marston reclining in his blankets under a wing.

That made me pretty sore. He knew the hour we were to start, and we had sent a man out to him with a vacuum bottle full of coffee and half a dozen buttered rolls for his breakfast. The messenger was standing alongside his car, smoking a cigaret.

I galloped over to George William, followed in order by Les and Bailey. Marston should have had the canvas covers off motors and cockpits, and everything ready for the warmup.

"Sorry to disturb your rest, Marston," I told him as we came within a few feet of him. "It's a shame to get you up before noon, but you can get your beauty sleep back at Langham."

By that time I was right over him, and as I looked down at him I saw that his face was a curious greenish color. His eyes glared up into mine with that non-stop hatred in them. Then, without a word, he staggered to his feet and over to one side of the field, where he had what looked like a paroxysm of coughing; apparently trying to vomit, but couldn't. Then he walked back to us, and seemed to be all right, temporarily.

"Sick?" I asked him, while curious onlookers gathered close.

"Get back where you belong!" yelled Les, and herded them away.

"I never was sicker in my life," stated Marston, mumbling his words.

"Any idea what made you so?"

"No, sir. Late last night a couple of fellows came out and gabbed a while, and finally went to town and got some sandwiches and coffee and we ate 'em. They beat it away, and I went to sleep a while and woke up sick as a dog. And I've been sick ever since."

"Haven't been drinking any of this moonshine?"

"No," he barked savagely, as if I was inferring that he was responsible for the war or something.

"Well, are you up to the trip?"

"Sure."

"The —— he is," stated Fernald. "He'd better find a doctor and lay up here a few days and meet us in Cleveland again for the next trip. He's as green as a drafted mountaineer, and——"

He was interrupted by another paroxysm on the part of George William. It was horrible to see his body wracked and wrenched around, without relieving the terrible nausea.

"Climb in one of those cars and get to a doctor as soon as we leave," I told him. "The next Martins'll be ready in five days. Meet us in Cleveland then."

He made no answer, but walked weakly over to the side of the field, and sat there numbly. Bailey primed both motors, and then Les in his ship and I in mine pressed the self-starter buttons, and soon the four great Libertys were roaring a diapason of power. I watched the maze of instruments—just double as many as in a single-motored ship, of course—and then idled my left motor while I gave the right one full gun, tried it on either switch of the double-ignition system, and listened carefully.

Everything was sweet as a nut, and the same procedure was gone through with the other motor. My ship was r'arin' to go, and so was Fernald's. The field guard pulled the blocks and tossed them into the rear cockpit, and I turned my ship on a dime by using only the left-hand motor, which pulled the ship around to the right. Then followed Fernald's huge Martin, like a house on wheels, up the field for the take-off.

The field lay practically east and west, and the western edge went right to the edge of the river. The wind was from the west. There was a screen of trees and undergrowth between the edge and the Ohio, the tops of the trees some fifteen feet above the level of the field. The growth was on the banks of the river, which sloped down from the field to the water.

As I was turning for the take-off Les, with Bailey beside him, gave his ship the guns. It roared away across the field, and in a moment his steady pressure on the wheel had the tail up. I waited, in order to give the air, which would be badly scrambled by the wash of two propellers, a chance to clear a bit. I set my goggles, jazzed each motor a bit, and shoved the two throttles all the way on just as Les left the ground.

In a Martin there is no obstruction to your view, the motors being to each side of you. It took all my strength, pushing against the wheel, to get the tail up. As my big bomber picked up speed Les was circling over the river.

Then two things happened simultaneously. I heard a wild mixture of yells, screams and shrieks from the cars drawn up on the edges of the field at the same moment that the tail of my ship hit the ground again with a terrific crunch and the wheel under my hands suddenly became free, as easily movable as if it was attached to nothing whatever. I took a split-second to look up, and saw Fernald's Martin, in a half-spin, drop below the edge of the trees. The next second a reversed Niagara of water rose above the foliage.

My brain, none too hardy an instrument at best, was literally as numb as a piece of sausage. But I could not think of Les then. My elevators were no more—that was why the wheel had become free in my hand and the tail back on the ground. I was within a hundred feet of the trees, traveling at more than fifty miles an hour, with no chance of taking off. In a flash my hand dropped to the throttles. By cutting one, the other motor would drag the ship around, probably wrecking a wing, but saving me.

Even as I did so, I knew I could not do it. For those —— cars had lined each edge of the field, and my ship would probably plow through them, killing every fool spectator in the bunch.

There was nothing to do but let it go straight ahead. It was slowing up, but four tons which has been going close to sixty miles an hour can't stop as quick as a motorless Ford going up Pike's Peak when the brakes are applied. As inevitably as fate itself, I was trundling swiftly toward those trees, with only a frail cockpit between myself and them, and two props to hem me in and keep me from jumping.

I cut the switches fifty feet from the trees. Up went my goggles, and off went my belt. I got to my feet on the seat the second before the ship plunged over the embankment. The trees were ten feet ahead. As it crashed over the lip of the field toward them I crouched, and leaped like a kangaroo. And by the seven thousand sweethearts of King Solomon I got my hands around a limb that swayed underneath me, and there I clung, like a monkey by its tail, thirty feet above the base of the tree.

Had I gone down with the ship all that would have remained of Slim Evans would have been an over-sized pancake. The four-ton ship crashed against the sturdy trees, and the observer's cockpit crumpled like an eggshell. The trees swept half through both wings, and at the finish one great oak was the exclusive occupant of the cockpit which had once been mine. I'd have been wrapped around it in loving embrace, never to leave it until they scraped me off.

I scrambled on this swaying reed of a limb, and worked my way back toward the trunk of the tree. I had no time for the fainting, screaming, yelling and generally hysterical bunch of nitwits on the field, but safe in a crotch of the tree gazed down upon the river. There was Fernald's Martin, half-submerged, and on the upflung tail was Mr. Fernald himself, accompanied by Mr. Bailey.

I was so relieved I let out a loud yelp. If I could talk as loud as that habitually we wouldn't have had to wire Washington at all.

Fernald, squatting like a frog on a lily pad, waved airily to me, clinging pensively to my perch in a tree.

"Don't mind if I leave this here for a while, do you Slim?" he inquired in his placid way. "Hurt?"

"Nope. How about you?"

"Bailey's got a broken rib, or maybe two or three or four," yelled Fernald. "Otherwise all present and accounted for. Looks to me as though there was dirty work along the river."

"I'll see about a boat for you," I told him, and started to climb down the tree toward the surging mob beneath me.

I oiled up the mental machinery and had it whirring away at a great rate before I got down. While still ten feet up I gave orders.

"Get back on the field and stay there," I told the crowd. "And I mean it. Beat it—fast! All but Marston! Wait a minute. Who's got a boat or knows of one?"

"I—I got one!" stuttered one red-faced man with a gray mustache of the vintage of 1850.

"Get at it quick?"

"Y-Yes."

"Get it and get out after the two men on the river—quick! Rest of you back on the field."

They obeyed pronto, talking to each other continuously and with no one listening to anybody else. I had a sort of a kind of a plan of procedure staked out by the time I got down and faced the scaredest, whitest, most shaken-up sergeant in the American or any other army.

"You're sicker now, I presume," I told him grimly.

Marston could not speak. His tongue seemed stuck to the roof of his mouth, and he was a truly pitiful sight, I suppose, had I had room for any pity in my mind.

I was about to launch forth on something, when one of the occasional sensible ideas I get seized the opportunity to make itself known to me. So I folded up my tongue and said curtly:

"My elevator controls went bad on the take-off. Looks to me like Fernald's went bad in the air, and it was just the grace of —— he was over the water, and only a few feet high. Help me with this fuselage."

Marston, as I said, was like a man in a trance. His weakness seemed to have been effectually scared out of him, and he didn't try to vomit once. Which gave me pause for thought, in itself. *He hadn't been in my ship.*

We looked at the elevators, which were absolutely undamaged. The control wires were attached to the little cabane struts above and below the great linen fins—but they hung loosely. Then I broke through the fuselage carefully, so that patching would be all that was necessary to repair it, and took a look inside. The tail-control cables go through the fuselage, and are not visible from the outside except at either end.

In a very few minutes the evidence was all before me. The cables had been filed inside. Not completely through, but nearly. The object was clear. The few unfiled strands of the cables were sufficiently strong to hold and work the elevators when the ship was on the ground. But when it picked up speed, and one commenced to use the things with all the force of the propeller blast, plus the speed of the ship, acting against the surfaces, the cable was not strong enough to hold.

I had been lucky, in a way, in that mine had been filed a bit too much and had broken before I was going at full speed. Les' had given way over the river. It was my guess that the perpetrator of the thing had hoped that the cables would hold for a while, and give way during the trip some time when the ship was going at an unusually fast pace, getting underneath a cloud or something like that. It didn't seem likely that he or they would want the wrecks to happen on the field.

Marston saw it, and he was a broken man. For a moment, that is. My eyes must have shown what was in my mind as they finally met his. He straightened like a shot, and his sullen, strained face suddenly flushed as red as fire. He stood there, daring me to say something, and hating me worse than ever because of what had happened. And as I stood there I was utterly convinced that I was looking at as low and rotten a murderer as one would meet in a tour of the United States, where most of the murderers are.

But I held my tongue, except to say—

"Sick or no sick, you're going in a boat with me and we'll look over Fernald's ship."

He didn't say ah, yes, or no; didn't expostulate, explain or try to clear himself. With a baleful glare in his eyes and a shadow on his heavy face he went with me in a Ford, driven by a kid who tried to break all speed records, and we got a boat a half mile away.

We met Fernald's party on the way. Fernald transfered to my flat-bottomed dreadnaught, while Bailey went on toward shore. The boy was white and sick, the freckles standing out on his face as if one was looking at them through a stereoscope. I just asked one question—

"Did you inspect these ships from tail to nose last night?"

"Yes, sir!" yelled Bailey, his eyes like those of a madman.

Then they sought Marston's and so did Fernald's, only Les was calmly curious and appraising, where the overwrought youngster was half insane.

"Beat it on, Bailey, and don't talk a word," I told him.

I told Les what I'd found. Marston brooded in one end of the boat while the Boundville veteran, rowing us, bent to his work and asked one question after another which never got answered.

Well, exactly the same things had been done to Fernald's ship as to mine.

"We'll talk when we get back," I told him, jerking my head toward Marston.

George William caught the gesture. A wild, leaping fire flamed in his eyes, and a shaking paw was extended toward me.

"I know what you'll do!" he snarled. "You've got me now, and you'll railroad me to Leavenworth, —— you!"

"Shut up, Marston!" I snapped. "Remember who you're talking to!"

There was a second of tension in that boat which was enough to make one's flesh crawl. Marston, his full face like a dark demon's, sat like a statue, arm still out-thrust toward me.

"Listen, Marston," I said quietly. "No one holds you responsible for this. My opinion is that the men who brought you coffee put dope of some kind in it; that you slept like the dead, while they did the work, and that what they put in the java is reponsible for you being sick. I don't like you, and I never did and never will, as a man, but you're a soldier with a good record, and as far as I'm concerned you're above suspicion."

His big body relaxed suddenly, as if he had gone suddenly limp. A queer look leaped into his eyes, a sort of calculating gleam, as it were.

"Don't get excited, Marston," Fernald advised him in his equable way. "You weren't supposed to stay up all night, anyway, with the ship after the usual sightseers had left. Nobody's hurt much. Don't lose your shirt or go wild."

"Yes, sir," mumbled the sergeant, and relapsed into his brooding.

When we reached shore I gave the orders.

"Go to town with Bailey, Marston, and get a doctor for him. Both of you go to bed at the hotel. You're still feeling bad. My orders are that you spend the day in bed."

"Yes, sir."

They trundled off in the same Ford which I had used, and then Fernald turned to me.

"What about it, Slim?"

"Open and shut," I told him. "It's as plain as the nose on my face, and that's no secret. In the first place, Marston, as you may know, got as high as major in the war. I was under him when I was a cadet, and he was a harsh martinet who made life miserable for every cadet. He hated me, and I returned it with interest.

"Just a couple of days ago, when I found him a sergeant, I took off the old blouse and bars and licked him to a frazzle just for old time's sake. He doesn't figure there's room enough in the whole world for the two of us. That cock-and-bull story about a couple of mountaineers driving in, and then bringing him coffee is transparent. He filed the wires."

"Maybe he'd file yours, and get out of riding because of pretended sickness, but he's got nothing against me," Les protested, his eyes resting thoughtfully on me.

"Wait a minute. I don't figure that getting rid of me was all there was to it. Marston was a major, shot back to a sergeant. That made him hate the whole Army, and the Air Service in particular. I've heard him call the Flying Corps a bunch of Boy Scouts, because we're all amateur soldiers even if we are veteran flyers.

"I can see the change in him. Notice how sullen and discouraged and brooding-like he is? And his life has probably been more or less —— since he got to be a sergeant, because a lot of men who were under him at Donovan Field probably have ridden him pretty hard."

"What the —— are you getting at?"

"Suppose he hates the Service. He knows that these bombing tests are going to make or break not only the American Air Service, but every other Air Service as well, doesn't he? If we sink battleships, we're pretty near the first line of defense, aren't we, and even Congress can see that we've got to grow into a big boy, can't they? And in order to carry bombs big enough to even have a chance to sink ships we've got to have plenty of Martin Bombers, haven't we? And if the Martin factory put out four bombers a week, which is all they can do, right up to the time of the tests we won't have more than enough, will we?

"And if we don't get Martins the tests will be off, won't they. And before the world we'll be labeled an unreliable branch of the Service, ships uncertain, can't even get them a few hundred miles to Langham, to say nothing of being sure they'd ever get a hundred miles out to sea to drop bombs.

"Suppose Marston has become so bitter that he's off his nut a little, and wants to crab the Air Service every way. If he could burn down the Martin factory the tests would be off, wouldn't they?

And he lied about being in bed at the time the fire happened, didn't he? He did get rid of the first two ships, holding us up several days, and now he's got rid of two more.

"He didn't figure the wrecks would happen so quickly. He figured we'd come down in the mountains somewhere, dead as doornails, with the ships so smashed up that no one could tell anything. And if he wasn't under suspicion at all, back at Langham, some fine night he could see to it that whatever ships finally got there, after you and I were grease spots on the side of a West Virginia mountain somewhere, could be destroyed some way— fire—anything."

Les took a long drag of his cigaret, and his steady eyes narrowed. Along the road, a hundred yards from the riverbank where we were standing, continuous lines of cars were passing. Several rowboats were out on the river, swarming around the gradually sinking Martin like waterbugs.

Finally he said slowly:

"By ——, it sounds right, Slim. He might be getting even with you and the Air Service at one swoop. But you're claiming, of course, that he's a nut. No sane man could cold-bloodedly do what he did to Bailey and me, anyway. Maybe to you."

"If he destroyed the ships at the field here, he'd be almost convicted before he started," I pointed out. "By his method, he figured on getting away free and clear."

"He's convicted now," Les returned.

"Sure, because the cables broke too quickly. But not, Les my boy, beyond the peradventure of a doubt, at that. In fact, we might be wrong. There may be some one or company or even country who wouldn't like to see these tests come off. Listen to my idea of how to proceed to nail Marston right to the cross."

Les listened, demurred a bit, argued, and finally we came to a decision. He finally agreed whole-heartedly with me on all points. The combination of circumstances was such as to make merely a cluster of coincidences seem very unlikely. Marston's past, and his present attitude; the fires at the Martin factory; the filed wires; and above all, the convenient sickness which made it impossible for him to go up in the crippled ships, all pointed one way.

Les stayed at Boundville to summon a wrecking crew from Dayton, salvage my ship, and likewise to watch Marston. I wired Washington and immediately hopped a train for that thriving village. I was met at the depot by a pop-eyed trio of high-ranking Air Service officials, was rushed to headquarters without an opportunity to scrub off the cinders, and in less than two minutes I was telling my wild and wooly yarn to the chief himself and six puzzled, scared and completely flabbergasted aides, assistants and adjutants. Having finished the story, I talked about Marston, not even deleting the fight. Following on, I submitted my scheme to them.

To make a long story short, at the end of three hours Chief Mallory got up from his chair, and paced up and down the floor silently for about a minute. He knows more about the Air Service, I sometimes think, than all the rest of the men in it put together. The bombing maneuvers were his brainchild, and he would be made, or broken, before the world by them.

He'd fought everything and everybody for three years, trying to get a chance for his young hellions to show what they could do, and he was pretty close to a temporary madman as he took in the full possibilities of what I had told him. Finally he whirled on me and said quickly—

"If we accept your procedure, Evans, you know what danger you'll be in?"

"Forwarned is forearmed, General," I told him. "I hate to run any chance of doing an injustice to Marston, and I'm leaning over backward so far that if I stubbed my toe I'd fall on my neck, simply because I don't want my personal prejudice against him to result in any possible injustice."

"I see," commented Mallory. "Gentlemen, we will proceed as Lieutenant Evans has suggested."

So I went back to Boundville, and with me came Colonel Feldmore, a spare, thin-faced, hard-boiled, genial and square old colonel who was in the Army before the Spanish-American war. Likewise, there sifted into town and out to Cleveland, various Secret Service men whose identity was known to nobody. Feldmore conducted an open investigation, and the Secret Service men started checking up on the two strange mountaineers, of whom Marston could give but a very vague description.

Feldmore took a half hour to give a tongue-lashing to Marston because he hadn't awakened, at least, when the vandals were about. But the careful impression built up by every one was that Marston was not suspected in the least of having had anything to do with filing the wires. He was exonerated. Of course, strictly speaking, he could have been punished for laxity while on guard.

But in guarding a ship, except in very particular and extraordinary cases, it is a custom of the Service merely to sleep out there for the purpose of keeping sightseers from climbing all over it. In many cases it isn't even guarded at all over night. Who'd want to tamper with an airplane? In moonshine country, or among people who have any possible reason for wanting to harm a ship or a flyer, careful guard is kept, of course. But ordinarily not any more than enough to guard a car.

Well, while the Secret Service men were snooping around Boundville and Cleveland, Marston, Fernald, a new mechanic named Gray, shipped on from Langham, and went back to Cleveland to bring the next shipment through. At the depot—Marston not knowing it, of course—was an operative to shadow him every minute.

Marston, as a matter of fact, was in rather a bad way. Despite the fact that he had been, as he thought, absolutely whitewashed, he looked more like a sick pup than ever. His physical sickness had disappeared within a few hours almost magically. But mentally he was an invalid still.

The Martin factory was heavily guarded, of course. The newspaper stories had been carefully taken care of; just a small item explaining my wreck as due to motor failure, and Fernald's as the result of a sharp downward current of air over the cool water, which is scientifically possible. No word of the filed wires had got about, nor any connection between the fires and the wrecks. Every laborer under suspicion, by the way, had proved an alibi; which, in a manner of speaking, strengthened the case against Marston. The operatives were tracing his movements the night of the fire, among other things.

One ship was ready to ramble when we got there, and it had machine-guns installed in the front observer's cockpit and also in the radio compartment in the rear of the bomb space. They had been shipped from Dayton, at my suggestion, to help guard the ships if necessary. I wired Washington, and was ordered to proceed with one ship and let Les follow when the second one was completed. Time was getting very precious, there were only two Martins at Langham, and practise must start very soon. Already the brigade would be four ships short—four fewer two-thousand pounders to help sink our battleship.

Marston and I took off bright and early one Wednesday morning. Just before we started I got word that Marston had made no suspicious moves while in Cleveland, had not even conversed with a stranger. Nevertheless I said to him just before we started—

"Ride in the front cockpit, will you Marston?"

It is less comfortable there than beside the pilot, for the folding observer's stool has no back to it. He looked at me with haggard eyes and seemed about to protest, but he said nothing.

The reason I put him there was to keep an eye on him. Marston, while he did not wear wings, could fly a bit. He had taken some instruction back at Donovan in the old days, just for the fun of it, I suppose. And if the man had it in for me the way I thought he did, I wanted to have him right before my optics at all times.

Lots of things can happen in a ship which those on the ground could never know. For instance, the left hand propeller tip whirled around right close to my head. Marston could grab me suddenly as

I was flying and shove my head just a few inches over the side of the cockpit, and said six-foot prop, traveling fifteen hundred times a minute, would have gone through that bony knot on the top of my spine like a buzzsaw would through a cream puff.

Then he could land the ship, maybe safely, and pretend to have cracked it up, thus again killing two birds with one stone. No one would know that my own carelessness had not killed me. I simply mention this as one of the many possibilities. So I put him in front of me, where he couldn't make a move without my seeing it, and I had a Colt handy to my hand—very handy.

With both twelve-cylinder Libertys well tuned up I taxied over the smooth field at the factory, and took off. Around and around that little slab of green we circled, getting altitude while Fernald, down below, alternately waved and then shook his head. Funny how the Air Service likes to kid by pretending to be sure a man's going to be killed every time he goes up.

Cleveland is a funny town from the air. It's very long, along the lakefront, and very thin the other way. It sprawls like a fat worm on the ground. A veritable network of railroads run out of it toward the south, so I set a compass course, synchronized my two motors, read the dizzying array of instruments, and settled back to watch Marston. I figured that, if we had allayed any ideas he might have that he was under suspicion, something might happen. Probably in Boundville again, but just a possibility of something else.

Well, it hit quick. I'll say it did.

We were roaring along over the large, smooth, many-colored Ohio fields, about twenty or thirty miles south of Cleveland, when I spied a ship coming toward us. It was far in the distance, coming from the south. I figured it was a Dayton ship, of course. As it came closer I identified it as a Jenny, one of the ninety horse-power, two-seated training ships which every cadet broke in on. I thought then that it was a civilian passenger-carrying crate, because no Dayton flyer would make a cross-country trip in a Jenny. It seems like walking compared to a D. H. or a scout.

Marston was sitting there in the nose of the ship, his hands on the machine-gun scarf-mount and his head resting on his hands. His broad, powerful back did not move at all, and he had never looked around. He had his goggles up, I noticed.

In a short time, approaching each other at around eighty miles an hour, the other ship was close to us. It was not an Army ship, for it was painted a bright yellow, and it flashed golden in the sun. It was coming toward us at an angle. That was natural. A Martin Bomber is quite a sight in the air, trundling along like an aerial lumber wagon. It's so heavy that it's fairly stable, and after one gets off the ground the wheel handles so easily a baby could work it, so I watched the other ship and flew my huge craft automatically.

The ship was possibly a hundred and fifty yards from us, coming at a slight angle, as I've said. It was perhaps fifty feet above us. Suddenly it banked a bit, and its new course brought it on a line parallel to ours, but it was pointed, of course, in the opposite direction. In a flash I caught sight of a double Lewis machine-gun, swung on a scarf-mount in the back cockpit.

As it sprayed its hail of lead I had nosed my big, loggy Martin over as far as it would go. At the same second Marston, I realized, had stiffened, spun half around, recovered, and was at his guns. They had got him— I saw the blood soaking one arm of his flying suit.

I threw my ship around as the equally slow, but much smaller, Jenny banked and flew back at right angles to us for another shot, from above and behind. I spun the wheel desperately, to get the Bomber's nose pointed toward the other ship. Subconsciously I realized that all my suspicions of Marston had been wrong. There was some gang trying to crab getting the Martins to Langham.

I was straightened around for them as the Jenny crossed above us, those wicked guns being sighted by the gunner in the rear. We were looking right up into their muzzles, a hundred feet away. Marston was on his knees, sighting too. If we were to get them, I *must* hold the ship in position for a moment more. It was shot for shot.

It was. I saw Marston's hand, a mass of blood, pull the trigger of his Lewis as a terrific impact made me cry out and seemed to pin me to the seat. Something crashed through my chest, and I felt as if I had been torn apart. As if in a dream I saw the Jenny spinning downward. Then, through blurred eyes that could not transfer to my brain what they saw, I saw a huge bulk looming above me. It looked as big as all the world. I knew the Martin was diving like mad for the ground, but my nerveless, groping fingers could not find the wheel. And I didn't care. In short, I went out like a light, my last remembrance being a torrent of blood flowing down over my body.

V

I came partly to, not entirely, in what looked like a hospital, and for two weeks I was so weak I couldn't even talk. In another week I was out of danger, and by the end of a month I knew I was in a Cleveland hospital. Then Les Fernald and Jim Tolley—Jim had taken my place as a ferry pilot—were allowed to see me.

"So you're going to get well! My, my!" grinned Fernald. "Can't the Air Service ever get rid of you?"

"I'm trying my best," I told him. "What happened after I passed out?"

"Marston got you out of the seat and took the wheel before your ship crashed. He was —— badly wounded himself, an artery severed, for one thing, but he flew the ship with one hand and held a handkerchief to your chest with another, flew back to Cleveland and landed. That Martin came in like a drunken duck, and he cracked the landing gear all to ——, then fainted in the ship."

"Is he alive?"

"Sure. But he'd about bled to death when he got here, and you'd have been as dead as the free silver issue if he hadn't——"

"Well I'll be ——!" was all that I could think of to say, and Les assured me that I was that already.

"Where's the sarge now?" was my next question.

"Oh, he got his strength back quick—wounds weren't as bad as yours—and he's in the hospital at Langham now."

"Well, have the sleuths unearthed anything?"

"Plenty, but not all," big, serious Tolley told me. "One of the men in the Jenny that fought you was alive, but he wouldn't say a word. They've arrested three more, though. Don't know whether what they've said so far is right."

"Come on—get out of here!" my jovial doctor interrupted at this stage, coming into the room. "Slim's still weak as a cup of tea. Tell him tomorrow, whatever it is."

Before I left the hospital Les, who visited me every trip, told me confidentially all that had happened. Hold your breath now, and prepare. I suppose you think that at the very least you're about to hear that all the countries of the world got together and concentrated their nefarious master-spies in Cleveland and Boundville, bent on the destruction of the American Air Service. Well, they didn't. There is no international ephillipsoppenheiming about to be indulged in by me.

With that out, you figure big business. It is always proper to blame Wall Street for everything from the earthquake in Japan to the fact that it didn't rain in the wheat-belt during July. Well, that's out, too. You might know that anything I was connected with would turn out to be a farce-comedy eventually. I had to lay back in my bed and laugh myself sick again when I heard it. If there'd been any bullets left in my carcass they'd have clinked together like a castenets.

The fact of the matter was that a wealthy, gentle, gray-haired old nut inventor—a man who'd evidently gone crazy trying to get a perpetual motion machine or something like that—was really responsible for the whole thing. He's safely ensconced in a lunatic asylum now, working on a mechanical flyswatter or something like that. The facts are approximately as follows:

This old fellow was a multimillionaire, and for years had been trying in his senile way to invent things. Finally he'd concentrated on the Air Service, and had been submitting to McCook Field all sorts of things from a motor run by gun powder to an automobile that turned into a ship, wings sprung out, a propeller attached to the front of the motor, and all that. Naturally, all his stuff was infinitely ridiculous. If you don't believe how many crack-brained inventors there are who submit perpetual motion machines and all that, ask an official of any big company, or the patent office. And McCook Field gets its share.

He had been a harmless old coot, although a nuisance. Well, when the bombing was broached, he set to work, and figured out a scheme to carry bombs, each bomb to be hung under an individual balloon which was to be filled with poison gas. Then there was some magnetic idea which would make the bomb and the balloon go straight for the battleship attracted by the steel in it. When the bomb hit, the balloon would burst and spread poison gas all over. The only thing he hadn't figured out was what would become of the pilot, except that he might jump into the middle of the ocean in a parachute.

This old bird was very patriotic, offering all his nutty ideas to the Government free and clear. Now comes the hitch. A soldier of fortune, named Gimbel, and reputedly—I never met him—a very keen, unscrupulous and strong-minded person, had attached himself to this old gentleman and worked him for a fairly comfortable living, suggesting newer and nuttier ideas and pretending to help him work on them at a comfortable salary.

The old boy trusted him a good deal, and was pretty strongly under the sway of said Gimbel. Gimbel had decided, evidently, that he wanted a big piece of change all in a lump, instead of putting up with the vagaries of the old boy for merely a stipend, so to speak. So he'd worked on the old boy's mind, helping him become convinced that there was a deep laid plot to keep the Government from taking advantage of this priceless method of bombing.

The inventor was absolutely certain, finally, that the Government was in the hands of traitors who were working deliberately to make the bombing tests a failure, or at least, not as successful as they could be. The Martin factory, Gimbel convinced him, had bribed high Government officials to make them turn down his invention so that they could sell a lot of very expensive ships.

Then Gimbel convinced him that, in view of the fine patriotic motives behind the scheme, it would be a good thing to get rid of the factory entirely, thus at one and the same time getting rid of a big business which was working against the country for their own ends, and forcing the country to use the balloons and bombs of the inventor, which, of course, would be tremendously successful.

Gimbel patriotically offered to burn the Martin factory, or in some way stop the use of Martins in the tests, for a consideration of three hundred thousand dollars to be paid him because of the risk. The old boy fell for it and, when the thing was broken up, was actually working about fifty men getting the magnetic apparatus ready, and had sent a letter to a prominent rubber company in Akron, warning them to be ready to furnish the Government at least thirty free balloons at a month's notice.

Gimbel, hot after the three hundred grand, had decided to carry on after the failure of his attempt to ignite the factory in Cleveland. He had assured the old boy that the wrecks in Boundville had been due to the rotten construction of the Martins, and did not plan to let him realize what he was actually doing.

You can see, by the methods used, how easy it would be to ruin enough ships *en route*, without being caught, they figured, to cause the bombing to be a bust that year. And that meant Gimbel's three hundred thousand. He had got the aged millionaire so completely *non compos mentis* that the poor old man considered it a holy crusade for the good of the country.

The way Gimbel was operating was this:

Two men had drifted to the field at Boundville, without anybody seeing them, chatted with Marston, and then suggested some coffee. They had doped it, so Marston slept like the dead and they came back and filed the wires. In the gang Gimbel had collected—three men, it appeared—there was one flyer. In some way they were informed when I left Cleveland—that would be simple enough—and their plan of shooting me down was a very good one.

The wreck would have been a total, soul-satisfying and complete catastrophe, of course, with four tons dropping a few thousand feet out of control. Fire would have been inevitable, and the chance of ever discovering, from two heaps of bones, that we had been shot would have been negligible. By the time it was decided the two flyers would have been safely away, anyhow.

They might have reported the wreck themselves, or landed, looked over the bones, and made certain that any tell-tale signs of bullets had disappeared before they did anything about reporting it. Any farmers around would have known nothing whatever about such technical matters, and guns can not be heard above the roar of motors.

On my way back to Langham, and for several hours before I started, I had a good chance to think over all that Marston had done. Desperately wounded as he was, he had had to climb from his cockpit over into mine, get the ship under control from the seat alongside me, leaning over to grasp the wheel, and then unbuckle my belt and heave me out of my seat.

Then he had probably slid into my seat himself, and in some way pulled my far from minute body up beside him. He had flown the bomber back into Cleveland, amateur as he was at airmanship, and stanched my wound and let his own bleed.

When I arrived at the field all the gang were there. The leading flyers of the border, the California fields and even from Panama, Hawaii and the Philippines, were on the job practising for the big chance. And Marston was still the hero of the field.

I got my flight back, and went to see him right away.

"Thanks, Marston," I said as we shook hands.

"Don't bother yourself, Lieutenant," he returned in his rasping voice.

The sullen look was gone, but otherwise he was the same. He wasn't any chunk of soft-soap by any means. But his grudge against the Army in general had disappeared, anyway. A little adulation will go a long, long way.

"You gave me a square deal when you might have ruined me," he went on without a smile, his light eyes staring belligerently into mine. "You gave me a chance. You're a man, Lieutenant, I'll say that for you. But as a soldier——"

I let him talk. We were alone. Then I talked.

"Same goes for you, Marston," I informed him. "You saved my life, and you proved yourself a —— good man. I admire you. But my personal opinion of you still goes. We'll get along. I'll give orders and you'll take 'em, and this is the last occasion for conversation on anything except business that we'll have."

"Yes, sir. Now about Number 14, I think she's ready for test."

And that was that.

Not only that, but it's about every bit of it, I guess. You probably thought I was going to make myself out a hero. Now you see how dumb I was. All wrong. Funny how I keep muddling through, getting dumber and dumber, seems like, every year. I'd like to report that Marston and I fell into each other's arms, and that he became my stanch friend and my man Friday and all that, but even in that this yarn is completely cockeyed, and isn't like it ought to be at all.

But that's the way things work out in real life, I guess. Marston and I respect each other, and it's nothing to his discredit that he doesn't like me. He can find several people who would say that disliking me was only another proof of his remarkable powers.

Occasionally, when the wind is in the east, I am a pessimist, and at those times—whisper it—I'm inclined to agree with those last-named folks.

And that *is* all of it.

www.ingramcontent.com/pod-product-compliance
Lightning Source LLC
LaVergne TN
LVHW041802190726
843493LV00008B/2749